SIMON & SCHUSTER BOOKS FOR YOUNG READERS
An imprint of Simon & Schuster Children's Publishing Division
1230 Avenue of the Americas, New York, New York 10020

First published in Great Britain in 2019 by Simon & Schuster UK Ltd. as *Ollie's Magic Bunny*
Published by arrangement with Simon & Schuster UK Ltd.
First US edition 2019

SIMON & SCHUSTER BOOKS FOR YOUNG READERS is a trademark of Simon & Schuster, Inc.
For information about special discounts for bulk purchases, please contact Simon & Schuster
Special Sales at 1-866-506-1949 or business@simonandschuster.com.
The Simon & Schuster Speakers Bureau can bring authors to your live event.
For more information or to book an event, contact the Simon & Schuster Speakers
Bureau at 1-866-248-3049 or visit our website at www.simonspeakers.com.
The text for this book was set in Corda.
Manufactured in China
1018 SUK
10 9 8 7 6 5 4 3 2 1
CIP data for this book is available from the Library of Congress.
ISBN 978-1-5344-3828-6
ISBN 978-1-5344-3829-3 (eBook)

THE
LITTLE RABBIT

Nicola Killen

A Paula Wiseman Book
Simon & Schuster Books for Young Readers
New York   London   Toronto   Sydney   New Delhi

Ollie and her toy bunny had been waiting for the rain to stop for a long, long time.

At last the day had arrived! They rushed to get ready—there were so many puddles outside to splash in!

Ollie spotted the perfect puddle right away, but before she could jump in . . .

Whooooosh!

A sudden breeze whistled past, bringing a cloud of blossom with it.

"Does that tickle, Bunny?" Ollie laughed.
A tiny petal had landed on his nose.

Bunny didn't answer, but
his nose began to twitch!

Ollie thought she must have
imagined it, but when she
looked again, Bunny's ears
were moving too!

Suddenly, he sprang from the basket
toward a group of rabbits playing chase!

"Wait for me!" Ollie cried ...

but the rabbits had soon raced out of sight.

"Bunny?" Ollie called softly.

"Bunny! Where are you?"

Her voice grew louder and louder
as she searched and searched.

But she couldn't find him.

Ollie was so worried, she didn't notice the dark clouds gathering overhead.

Just as she was wondering if she would ever see Bunny again, Ollie spotted something . . . and gasped!

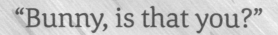

"Bunny, is that you?"

The water was rising and Bunny was in danger!
Ollie didn't know how to help.

Then she remembered her umbrella.

If only the magical breeze would blow again.
Ollie closed her eyes tightly and wished and wished . . .

Whooooosh!

She leaned out as far as she could, reached for Bunny, and grabbed him just in time.

"I'm so glad you're safe," she whispered.

But Bunny was very cold, and they needed to find shelter.

Pitter-patter,

pitter-patter,

pitter-patter.

When the rain finally stopped, Ollie knew
it was time to go home . . . she just didn't
know the way.

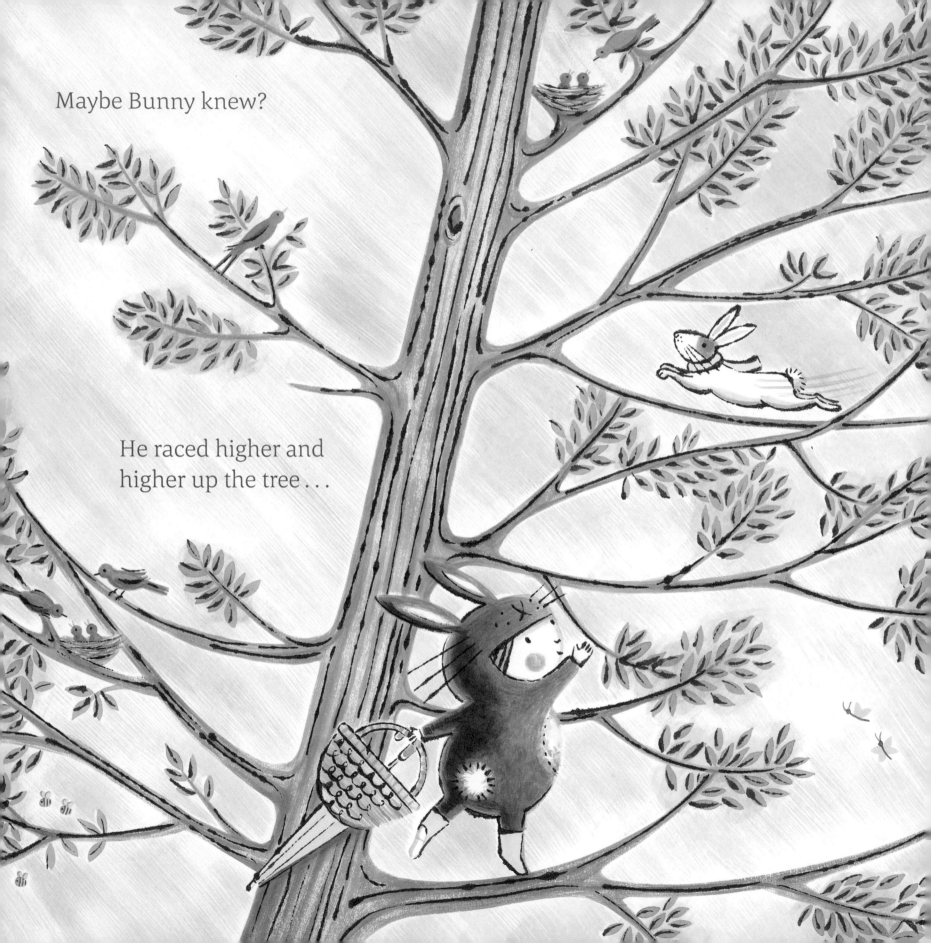

Maybe Bunny knew?

He raced higher and
higher up the tree . . .

until he reached the very top
and leaped onto a passing cloud!

What could Ollie do?

She took a deep breath, opened her umbrella . . .

and jumped too!

Ollie and Bunny floated through the sky, amazed by all the different clouds they could see, and how small everything looked below.

Then with a final...

Whooooosh!

The breeze brought them down toward home.

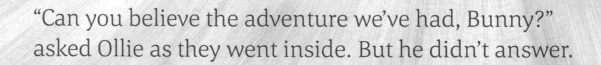

"Can you believe the adventure we've had, Bunny?"
asked Ollie as they went inside. But he didn't answer.

Ollie looked down and blinked.

Bunny was a toy again!

It was getting late, but there was just enough time for
Ollie to read Bunny a story before bed. She carefully
tucked his petal inside the book to keep it safe.

"Night night, Bunny," Ollie whispered sleepily.

Bunny didn't reply. But as Ollie's eyes closed,
she was sure she saw his nose twitch. . . .